THE BIG BAD STORY BOOK

You'll love reading all about
The Witch Who Loved to Make Children Cry
The Monster Who Couldn't Scare Anyone
and The Dragon Who Couldn't Help
Breathing Fire

stories by
Denis Bond

illustrated by
Valeria Petrone

Hippo

Also by Denis Bond and Valeria Petrone

The Train Who Was Frightened of the Dark
The Shark Who Bit Things He Shouldn't
The Granny Who Wasn't Like Other Grannies

To find out all about Denis's other books, take a look at:
http://freespace.virgin.net/denis

Scholastic Children's Books,
Commonwealth House, 1-19 New Oxford Street,
London WC1A 1NU, UK
a division of Scholastic Ltd

London ~ New York ~ Toronto ~ Sydney ~ Auckland
Mexico City ~ New Delhi ~ Hong Kong

The Witch Who Loved to Make Children Cry was first published by Scholastic Ltd in 1996
Text copyright © Denis Bond, 1996
Illustrations copyright © Valeria Petrone, 1996

The Monster Who Couldn't Scare Anyone was first published by Scholastic Ltd in 1994
Text copyright © Denis Bond, 1994
Illustrations copyright © Valeria Petrone, 1994

The Dragon Who Couldn't Help Breathing Fire was first published by Scholastic Ltd in 1990
Text copyright © Denis Bond, 1990
Illustrations copyright © Valeria Petrone, 1990

This omnibus edition first published by Scholastic Ltd, 2000

ISBN 0 439 99856 5

Printed in Dubai

All rights reserved

2 4 6 8 10 9 7 5 3 1

The Witch Who Loved To Make Children Cry

In a cottage, deep in a dark forest,
lived a witch.
She was a nasty old witch.
She loved to make children cry.

As the witch flew across the playground on her magic broomstick, she saw children playing.
"I'll go and spoil their fun," cackled the witch. "That'll make them cry."
The witch *loved* to make children cry.

The children were laughing
excitedly as they went round and
round on the huge roundabout.
The witch peered through the
railings at them and cackled loudly.
Then she pointed a long, bony
finger at them.

Suddenly, the roundabout began to speed up. It went *much* faster. *Very* fast. Far *too* fast.

"Help!" cried the terrified children, as they clung on tightly. "We're going to fall off!" Round and round went the roundabout. Round and round and round.

Much, much later, when the roundabout had finally stopped, the children staggered off. They were all feeling very sick. One small boy was crying. "Goody, goody, goody," laughed the witch. "That was great fun!"

The children angrily shook their fists at the witch, who WHOOSHED into the air on her broomstick. "She's always spoiling our fun!" grumbled a little girl.

Later that week, all the children gathered at the top of the hill for the kite competition. And as all the kites floated and danced in the gentle breeze, the little girl laughed excitedly. "Ours is the best kite here," she said.

"It most certainly is," agreed the judge as she strolled towards the children, carrying a shiny silver cup in her hand. She wanted to give the cup as a prize to the children who'd made this *beautiful* kite.

"Well done, children!" the judge shouted. "That must have first prize. It's the best kite here!"

"It *was* the best kite here," cackled the witch as she hovered overhead on her broomstick.

Then she pointed a long, bony finger into the air.

The gentle breeze suddenly turned into a strong gust of wind, startling everyone. And as all the children were lifted off their feet, they clung desperately to their kite strings. "Oh, no! It's the witch again!" screamed the small boy.

When the wind finally dropped,
everyone stared at their broken
kite strings.
There was no sign of any of the kites.
They'd all been blown away!
The children burst into tears . . .
which pleased the witch *enormously*!

"Please go away," pleaded the little girl. "Why are you doing this to us?"
"Aaaaah, have I made you cry?" asked the witch. Then she laughed. "Goody, goody, goody. I *love* to make children cry!"
And she ZOOMED off into the distance.

The next day, the witch perched in a tree in the children's garden. She watched them having a great time in their blow-up paddling pool. "I'll soon spoil their fun," she grinned as she pointed her long, bony finger at the paddling pool.

BANG! Hisssssss! went the paddling pool as it burst and went down.
The water and the children tumbled out on to the lawn.
"It's that witch again!" yelled the little girl.
"Why doesn't she leave us alone?" added the small boy.

The witch followed the children everywhere. She followed them to the park and watched them from the bushes as they spread out their picnic. "I hope she doesn't spoil our fun today," said the small boy as he nibbled on a peanut-butter sandwich. The witch pointed her long, bony finger towards the bright blue sky.

Suddenly, a large, black cloud appeared. With a flash of lightning and a crack of thunder, rain fell from the cloud, soaking the children . . . and their crisps . . . and their cakes . . . and their peanut-butter sandwiches.

The children hurried across the park,
carrying their picnic things.
Everyone, except the little girl, was
crying. *She* was very, very angry.
"We've got to stop her!" she shouted.
The witch watched them again.
"Aaaaah, they're crying again," she
said, softly. Then she laughed.
"Goody, goody, goody."

The children sheltered under
the old bandstand, waiting for the
rain to stop.
They saw the witch, leaning over
the railings of the duckpond.
She was happily feeding the ducks.
The witch didn't like children,
but she liked ducks.

When the witch turned around, she was horrified to see that her broomstick had gone. She ran along the banks of the duckpond, scaring the ducks and the geese and the swans.

"Where is it?" she screeched. "WHERE IS IT?"

The children sat in the bushes, giggling and watching the witch, who was frantically searching the rubbish bins for her lost broomstick. She looked very upset. "Serves her right," said the little girl, who was clutching the magic broomstick in her hand.

When the witch saw the park-keeper, sweeping the path with his very own broomstick, she rushed at him, angrily. "You've pinched my broomstick!" she yelled. "Give it back or I'll . . . I'll turn you into a frog!" The terrified park-keeper *immediately* handed it to her. He didn't want to be a frog!

The witch wanted to go home . . .
but the broomstick wouldn't fly.
She tried leaping with it from the
treetops. But first she landed in
the duckpond.

Then she landed in the sandpit.

Finally, she landed in a great pile of
smelly, squelchy manure.

The very sad witch had to travel home on the number nineteen bus. She was very wet. And she was covered in sand and smelly, squelchy manure.
Everyone stared and pointed at the strange, scruffy old woman.
One old man held his nose. "Ugh! What a terrible pong!" he said.

Back in the cottage, in the dark forest, the witch was getting ready for bed. "My broomstick has lost its magic," she said. "I'll never be able to do *witchy* things again!"
And she burst into tears.

Early next morning, the little girl, feeling very ashamed, arrived at the witch's door. Her dad was with her. "I'm sorry," said the little girl. "It's wrong to steal, so I've brought your broomstick back. But you really did upset us." The witch's face lit up. "Thank you for bringing it back!" she said. "*Thank you*. Goody, goody, goody."

That weekend, the children were riding on the very old merry-go-round horses at the fairground. Suddenly they heard a loud WHOOSH and a high-pitched CACKLE. Then they gasped in horror as they saw the witch ZOOM down from the sky.

"Oh, no," sighed the little girl.
"Here we go again!"
"Please! Please! Please!" cried the
small boy. "Go away. Leave us alone!"
The witch grinned, cackled again
and pointed her long, bony finger
at the merry-go-round . . .

Suddenly the horses turned into spaceships and flying saucers. They left the merry-go-round and sped upwards, where they WHOOSHED and VROOMED through the sky, miles above the fairground. "WHEEE!" shrieked the children, excitedly. "This is magic!"

And "WHEEE!" went the witch as she joined them, riding on a lightning bolt. "WHEEE! I never knew my magic could be such fun!" The children and the witch had a wonderful time as they ZOOMED and VROOMED across the sky. They laughed and laughed and laughed.

At the end of the day, as they all
tucked into enormous, magic-sized
ice-creams, the witch said sweetly,
"I *love* to make children laugh."
And as the delicious ice-cream
dribbled down her hairy chin, she
sighed, softly, "Mmmm . . . goody,
goody, goody."

The Monster
Who Couldn't
Scare Anyone

In the dusty bedroom of a large, empty house stood an old, iron bed. Under the old, iron bed there lived a monster. He was a very unhappy monster. He had nobody to scare.

During the day, he would stomp around the large, empty house making monster noises. "YUGGA! YUGGA!" But all the rooms were empty. There was no one to scare.

At night he would stomp through the weed-tangled garden, making eerie sounds. "YUGGA . . . OOO! YUGGA . . . OOO!" The owls and the bats took no notice. They weren't scared of monsters.

One moonlit night, when an owl
screeched, "WHOO! WHOO!"
the monster ran to hide behind a
large oak tree. He trembled from the
top of his head to the tips of his toes.
He was scared of owls!

Then . . . FLAP! FLAP! FLAP! a bat swept over the monster's head. The monster screamed and ran back to the large, empty house. He was scared of bats.

Next morning, the monster stared sadly through the dirty windows of the large, empty house. Then he saw a lorry pull up outside. People began unloading huge crates . . . and furniture . . . and curtains . . . and lots and lots of toys.

Later that day, as he peered over the banisters from the top landing, the monster spied a dad, a mum, a granny and a small boy. They were putting down rugs and filling the sitting-room with furniture.

"At last!" cried the monster. "Someone to scare!" And he raced down the stairs, crying, "YUGGA! YUGGA!"

"Look, everyone!" yelled the small boy. "A monster!"

"Go away, monster," tutted Granny. "Can't you see we're busy?"

That evening the monster crept up behind Mum and Dad, who were sitting on the sofa, watching the television.
"YUGGA! YUGGA!" he cried.

"Come and watch this programme,"
said Mum. "It's very funny."
The monster sat between Mum and
Dad and watched the television.
Mum and Dad laughed and laughed at
the programme. But the monster didn't
find it funny at all.

The programme was all about monsters who were scaring people. "What's so funny about *that*," grumbled the monster, as he slunk off to bed.

But the monster's old, iron bed had been removed, so he made his new home under the little boy's bed. During the night, the little boy woke up and began playing with his computer game under the bedclothes.

The monster slid out from under the
bed and stood and stared.
"YUGGA! YUGGA!" he growled.
Startled, the boy leapt from his bed,
with a sheet still over his head.
The monster fled screaming,
"HELP! HELP! There's a ghost in
that room!"

Early next morning, the monster plodded off to the kitchen to see if there was anything for breakfast. Granny was mopping the kitchen floor.

Granny was so busy, she didn't see
the monster standing there.
"YUGGA! YUGGA!" he shrieked.
"AARGH!" screamed Granny, as she
leapt into the air. Her wet mop landed
on the monster's head, covering him
in soapsuds.

Granny fell, bottom first, into her
bucket, as the soapy water sloshed
all over the kitchen floor.
Granny was furious.
Her very wet bottom was stuck
in the bucket.

Mum and Dad ran to help Granny.
As they struggled to pull the bucket
from Granny's bottom, the monster
crept away, feeling very ashamed.
He'd made Granny jump . . . but
she wasn't *scared* of him.

Later, Dad decided to dig the weed-tangled garden. He dug deep into the ground and scooped out a shovelful of mud. *Someone* was watching him!

The monster rushed up behind Dad.
He was about to shout, "YUGGA!
YUGGA!" when Dad threw the mud
over his shoulder.
The mud hit the monster, "SPLAT!"
covering him from head to toe.
"Whoops! Sorry!" laughed Dad.

As the mud-splatted, tearful monster
sat under the small boy's bed, Granny
handed him a glass of milk and a piece
of chocolate cake.
"Here," she said, kindly. "Your lunch."
The monster was surprised.

Granny, Mum and Dad and the small boy felt sorry for the monster who couldn't scare anyone. They decided to make him one of the family. They decorated the inside of the cupboard under the stairs and gave him his own room.

Wherever the family went, the monster went too. One day they took him on a train ride into town. The carriage was full and there was no seat for the monster.
But he didn't mind. He sat in the luggage rack.

They took him to a toyshop. All the
children pointed and stared.
"Look," they giggled. "A monster!"
None of them was scared. But *the
monster* was scared!
He didn't like the toy dragon.

They took him to see a film
about some witches.
Everyone loved the film.
But the monster thought it was
far too scary.

They even took him to a restaurant where they ate spaghetti. But as the tomato sauce dribbled down the monster's chin, he said, "This is very nice, but it must *stop*. I have to scare people. That's my job!"

So that night the monster hurtled around the kitchen rattling pots and pans. He slammed cupboard doors. And he bashed himself on the head with the lid from a biscuit tin. "That'll scare them!" he said.

But Mum and Dad
were sound asleep.

The little boy was
sound asleep.

And Granny was
sound asleep . . . and
snoring loudly.

Nobody had heard the monster.
He hadn't scared any of them.

The monster hurried into the sitting-room to see what else he could rattle and bang and bash.
But he got a terrible shock!
Someone was loading a big sack with all the family's belongings.
It was a burglar!
The monster was very, very angry.

"YUGGA! YUGGA!" he shouted. The terrified burglar screamed, "A MONSTER! HELP!" He dropped his sack and scrambled through the window. The monster was very happy. "I *can* do it!" he said, proudly.

The monster quietly closed the window and tiptoed around the room, putting back all the belongings.
He decided not to tell the family about the burglar.

After all, he didn't want to *scare* them.

The Dragon
Who Couldn't Help
Breathing Fire

In a small cave on the side of a
mountain, lived a dragon.
Nobody ever came to visit him.
He didn't have any friends at all.

Even the milkman refused to go near the cave. He always left the milk at the bottom of the path. Like everyone else from the village, the milkman was afraid of dragons.

One day the dragon decided to disguise himself. He put on some trousers and an old jacket. He stuck on a false moustache and placed a flat cap on his head.

"Nobody will know I'm a dragon now,"
he said as he set off towards the village.
"But I must remember not to laugh."
When the dragon laughed, he
always breathed fire.

The dragon strolled along the river
bank, where a man was fishing.
"Come and join me if you like," said
the man. "I've got a spare fishing rod."

All morning the dragon and the man sat, fishing. They chatted like old friends. The dragon felt so happy. Suddenly there was a tug on the man's fishing line.

Together they hauled their catch from the river, but it was nothing more than an old boot.
"What a silly looking fish," laughed the man.

But the dragon laughed too and a
sheet of flame shot from his mouth.
The man was terrified. He dropped
his fishing rod.
"You're . . . you're a dragon!"
he stammered.

The man ran away, shouting,
"A dragon! Help!"
A tear rolled down the dragon's face.
"But I wouldn't harm a fly," he said
to himself.

The dragon dried his tears and caught the next bus into the village. The bus was full and a little boy offered the dragon his seat.

The dragon sat behind a woman
who bounced her baby up and down on
her lap. The baby was pulling funny
faces and the dragon tried,
very hard, not to laugh.

But he just couldn't help it!
His laughter shot flames across the
heads of the passengers, sending them
all screaming from the bus.
The bus skidded to a halt.

The sad dragon walked the rest of the way to the village. As he passed shops selling all kinds of food, he began to feel very hungry.

Arriving at a tea-shop, he peered
through the window and saw people
tucking into sandwiches and cakes.
The dragon's tummy was rumbling,
but he had no money to buy food.

The waitress saw his nose pressed
up against the glass.
"Poor man," she said. "He looks
so hungry." She waved at him, but
the dragon thought she was shooing
him away.

As he was about to leave, the waitress rushed out of the tea-shop and grabbed the dragon's arm. "Come and sit down," she said. "I'll get you something to eat."

The waitress picked out a big cream cake for the dragon's tea. But as she brought it to the table, she tripped over a little old lady's handbag.

The waitress tumbled to the floor,
and when the customers saw her face,
all covered with thick, gooey cream,
they laughed and laughed. She looked
so funny.
The waitress laughed too.

The dragon tried hard not to laugh, but he just couldn't help it. Giant flames leapt towards the counter, where they burnt all the cakes and toasted all the sandwiches.

"I'm sorry," said the dragon, when he
saw what had happened.
But no-one was listening. Everyone
ran, screaming, from the tea-shop.
"It's a dragon! It's a dragon!
Help! Help!"

The tearful dragon decided to go home. He knew he'd never find a friend, because he just couldn't help breathing fire.
On the way to his cave, he passed a small cottage.

"Hello!" he heard a voice call, and a little old woman hurried from the cottage towards him.
"Don't come too near," he warned her, kindly. "I'm a dragon. I breathe fire."

"I don't care if you're a monster from outer-space," said the little old woman, "just so long as you can help me." And she pulled the dragon through her cottage door.

"My stove has gone out," explained the little old woman, "and I can't cook my dinner."
"I can light it for you," said the dragon. "But you'll have to make me laugh!"

The little old woman popped a
saucepan on her head and danced a
very funny dance around the kitchen.
But it wasn't funny enough to make
the dragon laugh.

She cartwheeled across the room,
singing silly songs and pulling
silly faces.
But still she couldn't make
the dragon laugh.

Then she had an idea. She grabbed
her feather duster and tickled under
the dragon's arm.
The dragon roared with laughter.
He was very ticklish.

With the flames that shot from his
mouth, the dragon lit the old
woman's stove.
"Would you like to stay for dinner?"
she asked. "There's plenty here
for two."

The dinner was delicious, and both
the dragon and the little old woman
had plenty to talk about.
"Will you come and see me again
tomorrow?" asked the little old woman.

A very happy dragon climbed into
bed that night.
"I've found a friend," he chuckled.
And as he did so, a tiny flame oozed
from the corner of his mouth.